JEFFREY AND
THE THIRD-GRADE GHOST
Max Onstage

Other Jeffrey and the Third-Grade Ghost Books

Jeffrey and the Third-Grade Ghost

BOOK FIVE

Max Onstage

Megan Stine
AND
H. William Stine

FAWCETT COLUMBINE
NEW YORK

JEFFREY AND
THE THIRD-GRADE GHOST
Max Onstage

Chapter One

"Don't forget to pack two desserts," Jeffrey Becker said to his father. Mr. Becker was fixing Jeffrey's school lunch. Jeffrey supervised from the breakfast table.

"*Two* desserts?" asked Mr. Becker. "Why do you need two desserts?"

For a moment, Jeffrey thought about telling the truth. "Well, Dad," he might say, "it's like this. One of my best friends is a ghost. His name is Max and he lives in my desk at school. Max goes crazy for desserts. So I want an extra one to share."

But if he told the truth, Jeffrey knew what his father would say. "Jeffrey," he'd say, "you've made up about a hundred thousand stories in your young life. But this one should win an award."

So instead, Jeffrey made up a story. "Well, you see, Dad, there's this new research that I read about in the newspaper. It said that ninety

3

percent of all college graduates ate two desserts every day when they were in the third grade. So I figure if I ever want to graduate from college, I'd better eat right, starting now."

"Jeffrey," Mr. Becker said, "you've made up about a hundred thousand stories in your young life. But this one should win an award."

"Not really, Dad," answered Jeffrey. "I'm still saving the best story for last."

Just then, there was a knock on the kitchen door. Melissa McKane, Jeffrey's next-door neighbor, rushed in. Right behind her was Jeffrey's best friend, Benjamin Hyde.

"Hi, Mr. Becker," Melissa said. "Hurry up, Jeffrey. We're three minutes behind schedule already. And I can't be late for school because we're choosing parts for the class play today."

"I've got it calculated," Ben said, looking at his new watch. Ben was going to be a scientist when he grew up. He liked things to be exact. "If we walk for three blocks, jog every other block, and then run like crazy for two blocks, we'll get to school on time."

"Okay. Let's go," Jeffrey said. "See ya, Dad."

Jeffrey's father smiled and dropped a second dessert into Jeffrey's lunch. He handed the bag to Jeffrey.

4

"Thanks!" Jeffrey called as he ran out the door. On the way to school, Jeffrey looked at the extra dessert in his lunch bag and thought about Max. It was great knowing a ghost—but it was lonely, too. Jeffrey wished he could tell his friends about Max. Especially his friend, Kenny.

"Hey, snap out of it," Ben said as they jogged onto the second block. "You have that faraway look on your face, Jeffrey. Like you're on another planet."

"It's a stage he's going through," Melissa said. "Ever since the beginning of the year. I think he has a crush on Mrs. Merrin."

Wrong, Jeffrey thought to himself. It's ever since I met Max in my desk at school. But he didn't say that to Melissa. "Melissa, why are you so worried about getting a part in the class play?" Jeffrey asked. "You're always picked to be the star and you know it."

"I know," Melissa said. "That's why I'm worried. Maybe Mrs. Merrin will think I've been the star too much, and she'll pick someone else."

"Is that so bad?" asked Ben.

"It would be terrible," Melissa said, "because my dad has never come to a class play before. And this year he promised to come."

Just then, a tiny alarm went off. Melissa looked at the beeping stopwatch that was hanging around her neck.

"Uh-oh. We've only got sixty seconds left!"

6

she yelled. And with that, she broke into a sprint, heading at top speed for school.

Jeffrey and Ben tried to keep up with her, but it was no use. Melissa's long red ponytail bobbed up and down and then disappeared around the corner at the end of the block. She was the fastest sprinter in the third grade.

When Jeffrey and Ben got to school, their other good friend, Kenny Thompsen, was still in the hallway. He was putting his jacket in his locker.

"Hi, Jeffrey," said Kenny.

"Hi," Jeffrey answered, panting and breathing hard.

"How come you guys are out of breath?" Kenny asked.

"Melissa made us run to school," Ben answered. "She wanted to get here early so she could talk to Mrs. Merrin. She really wants the leading part in the class play."

"So remember," Jeffrey teased Kenny, "no matter how much you want to, don't volunteer for the lead, okay?"

"Me?" Kenny said, laughing. "Are you kidding? I'm too shy to volunteer to sit in the audience."

"Yeah," Ben chimed in. "We don't have to

worry about Kenny. I don't think he's going to push Melissa out of the way and yell, 'Pick me! Pick me, Mrs. Merrin!' "

The three friends laughed.

"That's for sure," Jeffrey agreed. He started to go into the classroom, but Kenny grabbed his arm. "Jeffrey," he said in a low voice. "I have something important to ask you. When do I get to meet the ghost?"

Oh, no. Here we go again, Jeffrey thought. Ever since Pet Day, when Kenny saw some pretty strange things that Max did, he had been asking Jeffrey about the ghost. And Jeffrey wanted to tell him the truth. "Yes! There really is a third-grade ghost," Jeffrey would say. "He can make himself visible or invisible any time he wants, and he's funny, he talks weird, and he's a really good friend." It would be cool to let Kenny meet Max.

The only trouble was, Max wouldn't cooperate. He refused to show himself to anyone but Jeffrey.

"We'll talk about it tonight when you come for a sleep-over," Jeffrey told Kenny, trying to avoid giving a firm answer. Then he walked into the classroom and took his seat.

As soon as the second bell rang, Mrs. Merrin

sat down on the edge of her desk and said, "Let's talk about the class play. Now, as you can see, I've listed some ideas on the board. We could do a play about Christopher Columbus or one about the Vikings discovering America. Or we could do a play about Sir Isaac Newton, one of the most important early scientists. Or . . ."

Jeffrey tuned out and let his eyes quickly scan her list of ideas. Big trouble, he thought to himself. All of Mrs. Merrin's play ideas were about *men*! So how could Melissa be the star?

Jeffrey looked over at Melissa and saw that her face was filled with disappointment. There's got to be something I can do to help, Jeffrey thought. Maybe I can get Max involved! But first Jeffrey would have to get thrown out of class to do it.

Quickly Jeffrey reached into his desk and took out one of his desserts from his lunch bag. It was a piece of cake. He unwrapped it and started rubbing it furiously across his desk. In seconds his desk top was covered with sticky crumbs.

"Jeffrey!" Mrs. Merrin said, quickly pushing her round reading glasses back on her forehead. Her large blue eyes glared right at him. "Why are you doing that?"

"I have some ink on my desk and I was washing it off," Jeffrey replied.

"With your dessert?" Mrs. Merrin said, trying not to get angry.

"Why not?" asked Jeffrey. "It's a piece of *sponge* cake."

Everyone in class laughed. But Mrs. Merrin looked really angry now. "Jeffrey, stand in the hall until you're ready to be a part of this class," she said.

Jeffrey put on a sad face as he walked out of the classroom. But inside he was happy because his plan had worked. Now he had a chance to talk to Max.

"Max, where are you?" Jeffrey whispered.

A few locker doors rattled and then one of them opened. Slowly the ghost began to float out of it. At first Jeffrey could see right through Max. Then Max became solid-looking.

Jeffrey and the ghost were about the same height: four and a half feet. And they were the same age: almost nine. But Max looked and talked like a kid from the 1950s. He always dressed in baggy jeans with rolled-up cuffs, black high-tops, and plaid flannel shirts. He kept his long dark hair greased back, except for one curl that swooped over his forehead.

"Daddy-o, can't you get tossed out of class without, like, destroying my dessert?" asked the ghost.

"Max, I've got to talk to you," Jeffrey said. "Melissa wants to be the star in the class play. Only there are no parts for girls. Can you do something to help?"

"Daddy-o, like, I was groovin' on the idea that *I* would be the star of the play!" said the ghost. "But, okay, no sweat. She can star with me."

"Great," Jeffrey said. "Thanks."

"Is that all?" Max asked as he floated up toward the ceiling and stuck a piece of gum on the light fixture.

"Yeah, that's all. Why?"

"Well, for a minute, Daddy-o, I was shaking and quaking because I thought you were going to nag me about Kenny Thompsen."

"Well, Max, since you brought it up . . ." Jeffrey said.

"Like, not againsville," the ghost moaned, holding his ears.

"But, Max," Jeffrey insisted. "Ever since Kenny found out about you, he's been asking me once an hour to see you."

"Like, I'm hip to that fact, Daddy-o," said Max. "Because you've been asking me once

11

every *half* hour. Dragsville. Hey, have you ever thought about going greaseville with your hair? Daddy-o, it's so hip it's hop."

"Don't change the subject, Max," Jeffrey said. "This is tough. Finally one of my best friends believes me when I say I know a ghost. And you refuse to let him see you. He's going to get mad at me. And Kenny never gets mad at anyone. How about giving me a break, Max?"

"ABC," answered the ghost.

"Huh?" said Jeffrey.

"ABC, Daddy-o. Like it's been *A* real blast. I'll *B* back later, and *C* you around."

And, as usual, Max disappeared before Jeffrey could say anything.

"Jeffrey."

Jeffrey turned around and saw that Mrs. Merrin had come out into the hall.

"Jeffrey, I heard voices," she said.

"Uh, I was giving myself a good talking to," Jeffrey said quickly. Suddenly he started to scold himself. "Jeffrey, how could you do that to your desk? It was a really *crummy* thing to do. Are you going to behave from now on?"

"I'd prefer to handle that kind of scolding myself, if it's all right with you," Mrs. Merrin said with a slight smile.

12

"Sure," Jeffrey said. "You do it better, anyway."

"Thank you ... I think," Mrs. Merrin said. Then she shrugged. "Never mind about the cake. We're about to vote on the class play. Do you want to come in?"

Jeffrey nodded and followed Mrs. Merrin into the classroom. "For Jeffrey's benefit, would someone like to read the list of new ideas we've added to the board?" the teacher said.

Melissa's hand went up like a flag in superfast motion. Mrs. Merrin called on her.

"The ideas are: *Sir Isaac Newton*," began Melissa. *"The Vikings Discover America, The Pilgrim's First Food Fight ..."*

The class giggled.

"Melissa, just read what's written on the board," the teacher said calmly.

"I am, Mrs. Merrin."

This made everyone in the class giggle a little louder.

Mrs. Merrin stared at the blackboard and shook her head. Then she read the list out loud herself, picking up where Melissa left off. *"The Real Life Story of Elvis Presley?"* the teacher said. *"How to Blame Your Dog and Stay Out of Troublesville? Gross Things That Get Stuck Be-*

13

tween Your Teeth? Who wrote these ideas on the board?"

No one answered. But Jeffrey knew who had written them. It had to be Max!

"I think we have more than enough interesting ideas," Mrs. Merrin said as she erased the ones Max had added. "So let's just vote."

When the voting was done, the winner was a play about outer space. Melissa smiled because she knew that the star alien could be played by either a boy or a girl.

"Now," said Mrs. Merrin, "let's have a volunteer to be our star."

Almost before Mrs. Merrin finished her sentence, Kenny Thompsen's hand shot up in the air.

Jeffrey couldn't believe it—until he saw what had happened. Max was standing beside Kenny, *raising* his hand *for* him! Of course, no one except Jeffrey could see the ghost. Max just looked at Jeffrey and laughed.

"Kenny, I'm surprised—pleasantly surprised," Mrs. Merrin said. "And I'll be happy to give you the leading part. You'll be the star in our play about aliens from outer space."

Kenny's mouth flopped open and he couldn't say a word. He stared at his own arm, which was

still being held up in the air. Finally he turned
to Jeffrey. His face was pale and his voice was
shaky. "Jeffrey, help me. It's the ghost," Kenny
whispered. "He won't let go of my arm!"

Chapter Two

Throughout the rest of the day, Melissa glared at Kenny.

"Why is she mad at me?" Kenny complained during lunch. Melissa was giving him cold stares from across the cafeteria. "It's not my fault that Mrs. Merrin picked me for the play."

"I told you not to volunteer," Jeffrey said, although he knew Kenny hadn't really raised his hand himself.

"I didn't. It was the ghost!" Kenny insisted.

But Jeffrey just laughed. "Don't tell me. Tell Melissa. Only somehow I don't think she's going to believe you."

After school it was more of the same. Jeffrey, Kenny, and Max walked home together. Except Kenny didn't know that Max was there. Max was walking right alongside Kenny, grinning.

"Jeffrey, I couldn't put my hand down if I wanted to—and, believe me, I wanted to," Kenny said for the hundredth time. "Being the star of the class play is about the last thing I wanted. But the ghost made me do it."

"Daddy-o, this cat is talking about ghosts so much, like, *I'm* starting to get scared," Max said to Jeffrey. "Better tell him about volunteeritis."

·"Volunteeritis?" asked Jeffrey out loud.

"Volunteeritis?" Kenny repeated. "What's that, Jeffrey?"

"Uh, well, Kenny," Jeffrey said, pushing his brown hair out of his eyes, "I don't know if you're strong enough to take it. But I think you've got what doctors call volunteeritis."

"What's that?" asked Kenny. Kenny was always the first person to believe Jeffrey. And he was the last person to realize when Jeffrey was telling another story.

"Uh, it's a weird disease, that's what it is. It makes you raise your hand in class even when your brain doesn't want you to," Jeffrey explained. "I get special shots for it every year. That's why I never raise my hand to answer questions. I never volunteer to do extra work, either."

"That's true . . . you don't," Kenny said with amazement.

"Look," Jeffrey offered, "I'll prove it to you." Jeffrey cleared his throat and gave Max a small wink. He hoped that Max would take the hint. "Now watch this, Kenny. Who will volunteer to be dipped in hot peanut oil and rolled up in a giant taco shell?"

Kenny's hand shot straight up into the air. Max had grabbed his arm and raised it.

"Jeffrey, it's happening again!" Kenny shouted. "Someone made me raise my hand!"

"No, it's volunteeritis," Jeffrey said. "And you'd better watch out, because in your condition you'd even volunteer to spend spring vacation at the dentist's."

"You know what, Jeffrey?" Kenny said softly. "I don't care if I do have volunteeritis. Know why?"

"Why?" asked Jeffrey.

"Because if I didn't have volunteeritis, I wouldn't have raised my hand. And Mrs. Merrin wouldn't have called on me. And I wouldn't have gotten the lead in the play."

Jeffrey smiled at his friend. "It's pretty neat, isn't it?" he said.

Kenny nodded. "I've always been too scared even to be in a play before. Once I dreamed that I was in a school play. I was supposed to come out and say lots of things, but every time I opened my mouth bubbles came out instead of words."

"You're going to be fine," Jeffrey said. "And don't worry about Melissa. She'll get over being mad at you."

"And, Jeffrey," Kenny added, "I don't believe in volunteeritis one bit. I still think it was the ghost. And I'm going to prove it when I sleep over at your house tonight!"

That night, during his sleep-over at Jeffrey's house, Kenny thought he saw Max about a dozen times.

At dinner Kenny bumped his glass of milk and it spilled all over the dinner table. But he just laughed about it because he thought Max had done it.

Then the phone rang and it was a wrong number. But Kenny was sure it had been a call from Max.

After dinner Kenny started looking for Max in every closet in the house. Jeffrey followed him.

"Kenny, what are you doing?" Mrs. Becker asked when she found Kenny going into her bedroom closet.

"I read a book that said they're attracted to

cool, dark places," Kenny said as he dug around in Mrs. Becker's pile of shoes.

"What's he looking for?" Mrs. Becker asked Jeffrey quietly.

"Uh, mushrooms, Mom," Jeffrey answered.

Just then, Kenny came out of Mrs. Becker's closet. "Not in there," he said.

"Outside, Kenny," said Mrs. Becker. "That's where you'll find them."

"Really?" Kenny asked. "Okay, it's worth a try."

Kenny rushed out of the house and ran into the backyard to look for the ghost.

While Kenny was outside, Jeffrey went upstairs to his room and locked the door. "Max, listen to me. I've had it," he said. "You've got to let Kenny see you. He's going nuts and he's taking us all with him. Stop playing around. I mean it."

The ghost appeared quickly. "Like, okay, Daddy-o," said Max. "You've been totally patientsville. I guess it won't hurt me to say Howdy Doody to him—if it'll make you happy."

"Great!" Jeffrey said. He opened his window and shouted down to Kenny. "Kenny, come up here fast!"

A minute later, Kenny appeared in Jeffrey's doorway.

"Come on in, Kenny. He's here," Jeffrey said.

Kenny looked in every direction at once. "Where?"

"He's sitting on my bed," Jeffrey said. "Can't you see him? Come on, Max. You promised. Now do something!"

"No sweat, Daddy-o," Max said. He gave Kenny an invisible wave.

"Did you see that? Did you hear that?" asked Jeffrey.

"No, Jeffrey," Kenny said. "I didn't see anything and I don't think this is funny. You're really pushing your luck with this phony Max business. In fact, I'm not even sure I want to be your friend anymore, Jeffrey."

"Kenny, there really *is* a ghost on my bed," Jeffrey cried. "Just look! He's a third-grader like us, only he looks a little weird because he's from the 1950s."

"Like, who are you calling weirdsville, Daddy-o?" Max snapped at Jeffrey. "You're the cat who won't go greaseville with your hair."

"That's because I don't want an oil slick when I take a bath," Jeffrey answered back. "Come on, Max. You promised."

21

"Did I? Like, maybe I had my pinkerinos crossed, Daddy-o."

"That's not fair, Max," Jeffrey said.

"Sorry, Daddy-o. Gotta make like a banana and split," said the ghost. He opened the window and flew out.

Kenny watched the window open—and his mouth fell open. Then he stared at Jeffrey. For a minute he couldn't say anything. Finally he said in a weak voice, "Jeffrey, I take it all back. I believe you! This is great!"

Late that night, after talking for hours about the ghost, Jeffrey and Kenny finally went to bed. But Kenny couldn't sleep. He was too excited about the possibility of meeting a real ghost. He kept thinking about the window. With his own eyes he had seen it open by itself. And after it had, Kenny *knew* what he had wanted to believe with all his heart—there really was a Max!

Kenny started to ask Jeffrey another question about the ghost, but Jeffrey was out like a light. Jeffrey was the only kid Kenny knew who could fall asleep easily during a sleep-over. Oh, well, Kenny thought. I'll just keep my eyes open in case Max decides to come back. . . .

Suddenly, there was a noise in the hallway. Kenny sat straight up in his sleeping bag on the

floor. What if Max came back while Jeffrey was asleep? Kenny listened, holding very still. There was the noise again. He froze, and his heart pounded in his throat.

"Jeffrey," Kenny whispered. "I think he's here."

But Jeffrey just rolled over and snored.

Quietly, Kenny stood up and walked to the bedroom door.

Now the noise was coming from the stairs. Kenny followed it in the darkness. He wondered what the ghost was doing. Were there *other ghosts* with him? Would they be as friendly as Max?

The house was pitch black, but Kenny saw a shadow moving down the stairs and then into the living room. Kenny ran after it, taking the stairs two at a time. He followed the ghost through the living room, then into the kitchen. Finally Kenny couldn't stand it a second longer. As soon as he was close enough, he leaped.

"You're not getting away this time, Max!" Kenny shouted while in the air. He landed on the ghost hard.

"What on earth are you doing, Kenny?"

Uh-oh. That voice. It was so familiar!

In the moonlight, Kenny got his first look at the person lying on the kitchen floor. It was Jeffrey's father.

He had tackled Jeffrey's father!

Chapter Three

"I'm sorry, Mr. Becker," Kenny said. "I'm really sorry, Mr. Becker. I'm really, really sorry, Mr. Becker."

"Kenny, if you're so sorry, why are you still sitting on me?" asked Jeffrey's father. He was facedown on the kitchen floor with Kenny sitting on his back.

Kenny got up first and then Mr. Becker stood. He turned on the kitchen light. The milk he had been drinking just before Kenny jumped him had spilled all over him. And the raisin-cinnamon roll with icing he had been planning to eat was stuck flat to his pajama top.

"Kenny, I came down here to eat a late-night snack—not to wear one! What's your problem?"

"I'm incredibly, really sorry, Mr. Becker. I'm going to clean up all the spilled milk. Don't worry about a thing."

Mr. Becker didn't look as if he were ready to stop worrying. But he started to leave. "You know, when I had sleep-overs as a kid, we just stayed up late telling ghost stories."

"That's exactly what Jeffrey and I were doing," Kenny said.

After Jeffrey's father left, Kenny unrolled a big wad of paper towels and cleaned up the mess on the floor. But every now and then he stopped to look around. He had the feeling that he wasn't alone. "Max?" Kenny asked. The kitchen was silent. No one answered. "Nuts," said Kenny.

The next day, the entire class poured into the auditorium for the first rehearsal of their play. Everyone was excited about it. Even Melissa had stopped being mad at Kenny. How could she be angry when Mrs. Merrin had picked her to direct the play? It was Melissa's favorite kind of job—telling everyone what to do.

"Now remember, Kenny," Melissa explained, "you're from the Planet of a Thousand and One Commercials. You land on Earth with an important mission. You want to take some Earthlings back to be on a TV game show. Got it?"

"Sure," Kenny said.

"Okay," Melissa said. "Let's do it!"

Mrs. Merrin helped to quiet the class down to watch the rehearsal. Then Jeffrey and Ricky

Reyes came out onstage. Right behind them were Becky Singer, who was Melissa's best friend, and Brian Carr, who was no one's best friend. They walked slowly and acted as if they were afraid of something. This was especially good acting on Ricky Reyes's part because he wasn't afraid of anything.

"I thought I saw a spaceship land in those trees over there," Becky said in her clear, loud voice.

"I'll bet it's Martians," said Brian.

Ben, who was sitting in the front row of the auditorium, pulled his hair with his hands. "Brian, how many times do I have to tell you? It can't be a Martian because there is no life on Mars. Just stick to the script the way I wrote it."

"The way you wrote this script, flies could stick to it," Brian said with a mean laugh.

"Let's try it again," Melissa said.

Jeffrey, Ricky, Becky, and Brian went back and made their entrances again.

"I thought I saw a spaceship land in those trees over there," Becky repeated in her clear, loud voice.

Then Kenny walked out onstage.

Ricky, Becky, Jeffrey, and Brian all acted

scared of Kenny. But Kenny was the most scared of all, and he wasn't acting.

"It looks like an alien from another planet," Jeffrey said. "Where do you think it landed?" He pointed at Kenny.

It was Kenny's turn to say something. He looked out at the rows and rows of empty seats. His hands began to sweat. He was breathing too fast to talk.

"I said, It looks like an alien from another planet. Where do you think it landed?" Jeffrey said, even louder. Then he whispered, "Come on, Kenny. You can do it."

Kenny opened his mouth. He moved his lips. But nothing came out. He was too scared.

Melissa climbed up onto the stage to talk to Kenny. Jeffrey, Ricky, and Ben went over, too.

"Come on, Kenny," Melissa said. "Think positive."

"I had that dream again last night," Kenny told Jeffrey. "Bubbles were coming out of my mouth."

"That would be okay if this were a play about a bottle of club soda, but it's not," Ben said.

"Just remember," Jeffrey said, "some of the most famous people in the world have been shy."

28

Kenny looked at Jeffrey suspiciously. "Like who?"

"Like Christopher Columbus," Jeffrey answered. "After he discovered America, he became an inventor. He invented the telephone. But no one knows that because he was too shy to call anybody with it. So we had to wait another four hundred years for Alexander Graham Bell to invent it all over again."

"Is that scientific fact?" said Kenny.

Jeffrey crossed his heart.

"I'd like to see the book where it says so," Kenny said stubbornly.

"I loaned it to Ben," Jeffrey said quickly.

"Uh, I loaned it to Melissa," Ben added quickly.

"I loaned it to Ricky," Melissa said.

"Sorry, I used it in my karate class and split it in half," Ricky said.

The five friends laughed, even Kenny. "Thanks, you guys," he said. "I feel better. I think I can do it now."

But when they tried the scene again, Kenny got so nervous he couldn't speak.

"Why don't we try a different scene first, then come back to Kenny?" Mrs. Merrin called out.

"Good idea," agreed Melissa, the director.

So Kenny took a seat in the front row and Jeffrey found a seat in the back of the auditorium. Then some of the other kids began to rehearse their scenes.

Just as Jeffrey got comfortable, with his feet over the back of the seat in front of him, a voice underneath him said, "Hey, Daddy-o. Like, I was here first."

Suddenly Max appeared—and Jeffrey was *sitting* on him!

Jeffrey moved over to the next seat, but he didn't say anything to Max. He just crossed his arms and pretended to ignore the ghost.

"Like, am I digging a tantrum in tempersville, Daddy-o?" asked the ghost.

"You got it," answered Jeffrey. "I'm mad at you, Max. You never do anything I ask."

"Truthsville. But hey, that's like one of my grooviest qualities," the ghost said.

"No, it isn't. You promised you'd let Kenny see you and then you didn't do it."

"Next best thing, Daddy-o. Like, didn't I open the window in your room? And didn't I raise Kenny's hand for him? Kenny knows that I made the scene, even if he didn't lay his peepers on me."

"It's not the same thing," Jeffrey said.

30

"Well, I can't make a personal appearance for just any cat," Max said. "Maybe he'll think ghosts are cool, but, like, I'm total squaresville."

Jeffrey gave his friend a long, careful look. "You're afraid Kenny won't like you?" he asked.

"Something like that, Daddy-o."

"Well, Max," Jeffrey said kindly. "All I can say is, you won't know unless you try."

Just then, Mrs. Merrin called Jeffrey to come back up onstage. They were ready to rehearse Kenny's first scene again. As Jeffrey climbed onto the stage, he heard Mrs. Merrin having a private talk with Kenny.

"Kenny," she said quietly. "I want this to work out. I really do. But I also don't want you to be so uncomfortable. If you're still having trouble, we'll need to choose another alien. Someone with a loud, strong voice."

Kenny shook his head. "Nothing to worry about, Mrs. Merrin," he said. "I can handle it. I'll talk so loud you'll have to hold your ears."

"Good for you," the teacher said.

Then Becky Singer started the scene again. Jeffrey's line came next.

"It looks like an alien from another planet," Jeffrey said. "Where do you think it landed?"

Kenny opened his mouth to say his lines. He

was going to be able to do it this time. Everything was going to be fine. But just then Max appeared. He was flying and diving and zooming around the auditorium like an airplane. Jeffrey could see him. And he could tell from the look on Kenny's face that *Kenny* could see him, too!

"How's this?" Max called down to Jeffrey and Kenny. "Can you see me now, Daddy-o Number Two?"

Kenny just stood there staring up at the ceiling, unable to move or speak. He'd never seen a ghost before.

"Come on," Jeffrey whispered to Kenny. "Forget about Max. Say your lines."

"Hey, if he doesn't say something soon," Brian Carr said, "we'll be in the fourth grade before this play is over. What's he looking at, anyway?"

No one knew the answer to Brian's question, so no one said anything. They all just stared at Kenny, who was staring at Max.

"Hey, Daddy-o. Groove with your lines. Like, you can do it," Max said, giving Kenny a big thumbs-up.

Kenny tried to speak, but nothing came out. He was too surprised to say anything. He wanted to say, "Jeffrey, get your dumb ghost out of here! He's ruining my chance to star in this play!" But it was impossible. His tongue wouldn't work.

"Kenny?" Mrs. Merrin called from the front row. "Kenny? Are you going to say your lines?"

Kenny didn't even hear her. He was totally transfixed by Max, who was still zooming around the auditorium.

Finally Mrs. Merrin came up onto the stage. She put her arm around Kenny's shoulder. "Kenny," she said, "I don't think this is working out. But please don't feel bad. Stage fright can happen to anyone. However, I'm going to have to ask someone else to be the alien. Let's see now. I think Brian Carr should have the leading part in our class play."

Brian Carr? The complainer? The one kid in the class who was never nice to anyone? Right then, Kenny wished that *he* were a ghost, so he could sink into the floor and disappear!

33

Chapter Four

Kenny looked at his teacher. Had she really given his part to Brian Carr, the most obnoxious kid in the third grade?

"Hey, thanks, Mrs. Merrin," Brian Carr said. "Now we're getting somewhere."

"And, Kenny . . ." Mrs. Merrin said in her softest voice.

But Kenny didn't let her finish. "Who cares?" he shouted. He pushed past everyone and ran out of the auditorium.

"Mrs. Merrin, you shouldn't have given the part to Brian," Jeffrey said. "Kenny was going to say his lines. He's just superpolite. He was waiting for everyone to stop talking before he started."

"The little geek was staring like someone pushed his pause button for twenty minutes," Brian Carr said.

Jeffrey glared at Brian. "Brian, in a recent survey of poisonous snakes, nine out of ten said they'd rather starve to death than bite you." Jeffrey ran out of the auditorium, too.

He found Kenny outside of their classroom. He was wearing his jacket and taking everything out of his locker.

"Kenny, what are you doing? School's not over for three more months," Jeffrey said.

"It is for me," Kenny told him. "I plan to be sick and stay home from now until after the class play." He slammed his locker door closed. "This is all your fault, Jeffrey Becker, and I want you to know we're playing with new rules now.

"Rule number one: You and I don't talk to each other. And the only time I'll break that rule is for rule number two: to say hurtful things to you."

"Hurtful things?" Jeffrey smiled. "Kenny, you're lousy at being mean. You didn't even know how to call anyone names until I taught you in kindergarten. And you still haven't really caught on."

"I'm catching on. Five minutes ago I was the star of the class play. It was great. And now I'm not. It's all your fault. You and that . . . that . . ."

Kenny was stuck trying to think of a mean word, so Jeffrey suggested one. "Try stupid."

"Thanks. You and that stupid ghost of yours ruined everything," Kenny said.

"But I'm mad at Max, too," Jeffrey explained. "I didn't tell him to go up there and scare you. I just wanted him to say hello."

"He said hello, and now I'm saying good-bye." Kenny turned and started to walk away.

"Wait!" Jeffrey called. "There's something in your locker." Jeffrey pointed to a folded piece of paper that was hanging half in and half out of the vent on Kenny's locker.

"Did you put that there?" asked Kenny, taking the note.

Jeffrey shook his head. "What does it say?"

Kenny read the note and then showed it to Jeffrey. It read:

The big pine tree in the park at four o'clock.
I'll make the scene. Be there or be square.
Stay cool,
Max

"Is this another trick?" Kenny asked.

Jeffrey shrugged his shoulders. "There's only one way to find out."

36

At four o'clock that day Kenny and Jeffrey waited under the big pine tree in the park across from the school. It was a huge tree that little kids always decorated with ornaments for Christmas, and high school kids always decorated with toilet paper on the last day of school. But Max was nowhere to be found.

"He's late," Kenny said at four-thirty.

"He's Max," Jeffrey answered.

The two friends sat down under the tree and waited. A pine cone fell from above and hit the ground next to Jeffrey. Then one dropped and hit Kenny on the head.

"Ouch," said Kenny, mostly because it surprised him.

Suddenly it started raining pine cones, lots of them. They were falling everywhere—around the boys, behind them, and on their heads.

"I think Max is here now!" Jeffrey shouted.

"Hey, listen!" Kenny said. "The pine cones are laughing."

For a moment, it did sound as if the pine cones were laughing as they fell. But Jeffrey quickly recognized Max's laugh. Then the ghost began to take shape, starting with his black high-top sneakers and working his way up to the slicked black curl that fell over onto his forehead.

"What's shaking, Daddy-o?" Max said to Jeffrey. Then he looked at Kenny. "Close your mouth, Kenny. Flies are getting in. Hey, man, like, I'm hip to what you're thinking in that empty hallway between your ears. You're thinking what a total gas it is to finally groove your eyeballs on me."

Kenny tried to talk, but it came out like silly laughing instead. "This is awesome!" He walked around Max.

"Hey, like, I'm not a Maypole, Daddy-o."

"I can't believe this is happening," Kenny said. "You're really talking to me. Can I touch you?" He reached out to move his hand through the ghost.

"Ouch!" Max shouted suddenly.

Kenny jerked his hand back, but then the ghost laughed.

"Ha ha ha! Two for flinching!" Max said. He flew around Kenny, floating on his back as if he were in a swimming pool.

"Uh, Max, uh . . . I don't know what to ask first. Uh, what does it feel like to be a ghost?" Kenny asked.

"Like, dig this. Have you ever put your face in a bowl of applesauce?" asked Max.

"Probably when I was a baby," Kenny said.

38

"Well, it doesn't feel anything like that, Daddy-o. Ha ha ha!" said Max.

Jeffrey looked at Kenny and shrugged.

"Wow! You can fly, you can make yourself invisible—you can go anywhere and no one would know!" Kenny was so excited he was almost shouting. "You could see what the president of the United States has for a midnight snack."

"Raspberry ice cream, last time I previewed the situation," said the ghost, buffing his fingernails on his shirt.

"I mean, could you find out what the Chicago Cubs lineup is for the next game?"

"Again?" The ghost sounded bored. "I already did that twice today."

Kenny suddenly calmed down as he got the best idea of all. "Max, I'll bet you could even make Brian Carr sorry that he got *my part* in the class play."

The third-grade ghost smiled. "Now that's one groovy idea."

"Gee. Would you really do it, Max?"

"Like, I could take care of that little detail right nowsville and still have time left for some B-ball action," the ghost boasted.

"Wow!" Kenny said. "I know where to find

39

Brian. He goes to the ice cream shop every day."

"All right!" Max said. "What do you say the threesome of us make the scene at the ice cream shop and groove on the goodies?"

"Sounds coolsville to me," Kenny said.

The ghost wrapped an arm around Kenny's neck. "I dig this cat. He's a speedo learner."

So the three friends went to the Sweet Truth Ice Cream Shop. It was just a short walk from the park.

The store was always crowded after school because in addition to ice cream, it also had a huge selection of candy in tall glass jars.

"See, I was right," Kenny said as they entered the shop. "There's Brian." Kenny pointed to a booth where Brian was sitting. He had a large banana split in front of him.

"Okay, Daddy-o Number Two, here's what you do. Just go over to Brian's table and tell him that you dig him the least."

"You mean you want *me* to start an argument with Brian Carr?" Kenny asked. He looked at Max with alarm.

"Daddy-o, Daddy-o, someone's sent your brain on vacation and I'm so saddy-o," said Max. "Not an argument, Kenny. I want you to start a *fight*."

"With Brian Carr?" Kenny said. "He'll total me."

"Not this time," Max said with a laugh. "Because, like, you're going to *start* the fight, but *I'll* finish it. Dig?"

"Yeah," Kenny said, smiling.

"Now while you're doing the deed you gotta do," Max said, "I'm going to make myself a super-double-duper-dip milkshake." And Max floated off behind the ice cream counter.

"This is going to be neat, Jeffrey," Kenny said.

Jeffrey looked at his friend. "You'd better be careful."

"No sweat," Kenny said. "I've got friends in invisible places."

Kenny walked over to Brian. "Hi, Brian."

"Hi there, carpet tongue. I see you finally got the fuzz out of your mouth."

"Brian, I just want you to know something," Kenny said. "I hate the fact that you got my part in the class play. And I'm going to do everything I can to get it back."

"The only problem with that," Brian said, "is it's a *speaking* part." He laughed meanly.

Meanwhile, the milkshake mixer started up loudly. Everyone in the ice cream shop thought it had started by itself. But Kenny and Jeffrey knew better.

"Yeah, well, I have to admit you're perfect to play the part of an alien," Kenny said. "Because you certainly aren't a human being."

Brian stood up quickly. "You're going to be sorry that you ever learned to talk!" he growled as he moved in on Kenny.

"Okay, Max," Kenny called out. "I think it's time."

Kenny expected to hear the milkshake mixer turn off. He expected to see the ghost fly over and handle Brian Carr. But instead Brian picked up his half-eaten banana split and dumped it on Kenny's head. And he didn't wait to see the vanilla, blueberry, and marble crunch ice cream or the butterscotch, strawberry, and fudge syrups run down Kenny's hair and shirt. Brian just left.

Finally the milkshake mixer stopped. Max came over sipping his milkshake with a long straw.

"Max, what happened to you?" Kenny asked angrily. He was dripping with goo.

"I don't know, Daddy-o," said the ghost. "I think I used too much ice cream. Milkshakes are groovy, but they're, like, tricky to make."

"Thanks for nothing, Max," Jeffrey said, glaring at the ghost.

"Like, don't sweat Brian Carr," Max told him. "Maybe Kenny got cooled off, but, like, I'm just getting warmed up!"

Chapter Five

It was always hard for Jeffrey to stay mad at Max. And now it was hard for Kenny, too. Even though Max was undependable, unpredictable, and unreliable—what Jeffrey called the three *un*'s—he was definitely *not* uncool. Kenny liked Max, and he wanted to be Max's friend. So he forgave Max for letting Brian Carr dump ice cream all over him on Friday afternoon.

The following Monday, however, Kenny expected Max to make good on his promise to help him get his part back in the class play.

Kenny got to school just before the final bell. He met Jeffrey coming out of the class.

"Where are you going, Jeffrey?" Kenny asked, following Jeffrey to his locker.

"I'm going home," Jeffrey said, taking out his jacket.

"You've been thrown out of school? It's only eight-forty-five in the morning!" Kenny was shocked.

"I wasn't thrown out of school. I'm going back home for my squirt gun, a can of my dad's shaving cream, and my nose glasses," Jeffrey explained—although it wasn't much of an explanation as far as Kenny was concerned. "Mrs. Merrin is sick. She isn't here. We have a substitute."

Kenny smiled. Even for a shy guy like Kenny, the word *substitute* had a special magic. It meant no quizzes, no homework, no rules. Instead, it was time to party!

"Come on, let's go get our stuff," Jeffrey said.

"Jeffrey, we can't just leave school and come back later," Kenny said.

"Sure we can," Jeffrey said confidently. "We'll tell the substitute that we were born in California, so we go by a different time zone."

Just then Max floated by carrying a squirt gun and a can of shaving cream and wearing nose glasses. "Let's go, cats. Like, I'm ready for class."

"Max," said Kenny, "we have a substitute today."

"I'm hip. And I'm here to help you guys flip out the substitute teacher. It's like our duty as students, cats," Max said.

"But what about Brian Carr?" Kenny asked. "You have to help me get my part back from him."

"Sure thing, Daddy-o," Max said. "But not today. Today I'm going to show you how *I* used to handle substitute teachers when I was in the third grade. I was a gas and a half."

The substitute was a young guy named Mr. Alexander. "But you can call me Earl," he told the class.

Max winked at Jeffrey and Kenny. "He's a pushover. Watch my superswitcheroo on the roll call."

Earl picked up a list of names—a list that Max had written. "I'm going to call the roll, so just yell out when you hear your name," said the substitute. "Ben Dover? Ben, are you here? Not here today. How about Otto Mechanic? Mabel Syrup? Russell Cows? Penny Loafer?" Earl kept reading Max's list of phony names until the class was giggling so hard that he finally caught on.

Jeffrey took out a piece of paper of his own. This one was for keeping score. So far it was Substitute—0, Class—1. Then Jeffrey suddenly called out, "Switch!"

Immediately, everyone in the class got up and moved to a different seat.

Earl frowned. "Very funny, you guys. Now take out some paper and a pencil and let's have a spelling test."

"Test?" Max said. "Daddy-o, you'd better do something fast. Like, when I was in school I never let a substitute give me a test."

"Earl," Jeffrey interrupted, "what about our snack?"

"Snack?" said Earl. "Aren't you guys a little old to be having a snack in school?"

"No," Jeffrey said. "We always have a nine o'clock snack."

"Oh, okay," said Earl.

"Sure, and don't worry about a thing, Earl," Jeffrey said. "We'll tell you what our schedule is."

After the nine o'clock snack, the class had recess. Then it was time for the ten o'clock snack, which led into free time and then another recess. By then it was time for lunch. At the end of the day, the score was Substitute—0, Class—23.

As Jeffrey and his friends walked home after school, Jeffrey sighed. "Boy, school should be like that every day."

"But we didn't practice our school play," Melissa said.

"We'll have time for that tomorrow," Jeffrey said.

"We'd better," Kenny said. "Because I want to get my part back."

"But what if Earl comes back tomorrow?" asked Ben.

A substitute, come back for a second day? That was the worst thing that could possibly happen.

"On the second day, substitutes won't let you get away with anything," Kenny said glumly.

"Yeah. And on the second day they know kids' names—especially the names of the people they had to send out in the hall a couple of dozen times," Melissa said, poking Jeffrey.

"Guys, be logical," Jeffrey pleaded. "What substitute in his right mind would want to come back to our class tomorrow?"

"Jeffrey, this is what I want to know," said Ricky. "How did you manage to put feathers in

Earl's cold chicken sandwich? That was so cool."

Jeffrey couldn't really take the credit for that. Finding Earl's lunch and putting the feathers into it had been one of Max's tricks. But Jeffrey couldn't tell that to Ricky. "It wasn't me," Jeffrey said. "It must have been the bread he used. You know, it was light as a feather."

The next day, Earl did not come back to Mrs. Merrin's class. Instead there was a small elderly woman with white hair and thick glasses. She had a cane that she used to rap on the floor for quiet and to point at kids who ignored her. She also seemed very forgetful.

"Well, they certainly have changed this school since I taught here," said the substitute whose name was Mrs. Scott. "I spoke to your teacher, Mrs., uh, Mrs. Martin . . ."

"Mrs. Merrin," the class said.

"I know that," said Mrs. Scott, sounding a bit cross.

Jeffrey knew it wasn't going to be very hard to drive this substitute nuts. It wasn't that far a drive to get there! And just wait until Max gets here, Jeffrey thought.

"Your teacher told me what she wanted you to do in class today. So please get busy right away," announced Mrs. Scott.

49

"But, Mrs. Scott," asked Ben Hyde, "how can we get busy? You haven't told us what the assignment is."

"I know that," Mrs. Scott said. "We're going to do some math first." She drew a large square on the chalkboard. "Let's say this is somebody's backyard with a fence around it. One side of the fence is thirty yards long. The other side is twenty yards long. Now if we filled this yard up with people, how many people do you think could play here?"

"One and a half," said Jeffrey, without raising his hand.

"Why do you think only one and a half people could fit in that yard?" asked Mrs. Scott. "This is a very big backyard."

"Because everyone knows there are only *three feet* in every *yard*," said Jeffrey.

Mrs. Scott looked at Jeffrey over her thick glasses. "You know, young man, you remind me of someone—although I can't remember who. Now can anyone else answer this problem?"

While the rest of the class thought about the math problem, Jeffrey looked out the window. I wonder who I remind her of, Jeffrey thought to himself. She's so old, maybe it's Abraham Lincoln. I'll bet he was in her third-grade class.

Suddenly Max appeared, slipping in under a window that was open only a crack.

"Hey, Daddy-o," he said to Jeffrey. "What's shaking?" Then Max suddenly stopped. He froze in his tracks. His face looked as though *he* had seen a ghost! "What's . . . like, what's Mrs. Scott doing here?" Max asked. But he didn't wait for an answer. He just flew out the window, calling, "See you later, alligators."

For a minute Jeffrey was puzzled. Why was Max running—or rather flying—away? And how did he know Mrs. Scott?

Then Jeffrey started thinking about the things Mrs. Scott had said. And suddenly it came to him. Maybe Mrs. Scott had taught at this school when Max was alive! Maybe that's why Max had been in such a hurry to leave. If so, this was Jeffrey's chance to find out the truth about Max!

During recess, everyone ran out of the classroom as fast as they could. But Jeffrey stayed behind to talk to the teacher.

"Mrs. Scott, did you teach here a long time ago?" Jeffrey asked.

"Yes," the older woman said. "Of course the school wasn't called Redwood then. It was called . . . it was called . . ."

"Bragaw Elementary School," Jeffrey said.

"I know that," Mrs. Scott replied. "But how did you know? It was a long time ago."

"I think I know someone who went to school here then," Jeffrey said. "Maybe you knew him."

"I don't think so. No, I've never heard of him," Mrs. Scott said with a shake of her head.

"I haven't told you his name yet," Jeffrey said.

"I know that."

"His name was Max," said Jeffrey.

The elderly woman took off her glasses and stared at Jeffrey. "No, his name was Maxwell. And *that's* who you remind me of!"

Jeffrey couldn't believe it. He was right! Mrs.

Scott had been Max's third-grade teacher! "You remember him?" he said.

"There are some students you never forget . . . no matter how hard you try," Mrs. Scott replied. "He was such a prankster. Do you know, one day he put feathers in my cold chicken sandwich."

Jeffrey smiled. But then he got ready to ask the big question. This was his chance to find out how Max had died. But did Jeffrey *really* want to know?

"Mrs. Scott," he began slowly. "Didn't something happen to Max while he was in your class? Something . . . terrible?"

"Why, yes." Mrs. Scott's eyes got a faraway look in them. "Something did happen."

Jeffrey waited for her to tell him what it was. And waited. And waited. Was she going to say it or not?

"But you know," the older woman finally said when her mind came back to the classroom, "I can't for the life of me remember what it was!"

Jeffrey sighed with relief. He realized he didn't really want to know. It was better for Max to remain just what he was: a wonderful, strange, funny, and *mysterious* ghost!

Chapter Six

For the rest of the week Mrs. Scott was the substitute teacher. And Jeffrey soon found out that although she had a bad memory, she knew how to get organized. She made a seating chart so that she would know everyone's name. She got a list of homework assignments from Mrs. Merrin. And she made certain that the class did them. So it was back to work for the third grade.

The other thing Mrs. Scott did was to chase Max out of the classroom—even though she didn't know she had done it. Jeffrey wanted to get the ghost and his third-grade teacher back together again. However, this was not possible, according to Max.

"Don't bug me, Daddy-o. Like, there is absolutely no way on this or any other planet that yours truly is going to make that scene," said the ghost. "She'd lay a month of detentions on me just for old timesville."

"But, Max, you're a ghost," argued Jeffrey.

"That wouldn't stop her," Max said.

So Jeffrey had to settle for teasing Max by calling him Maxwell.

Meanwhile, Brian Carr did everything he could to make Kenny feel bad about losing the part in the class play. And he started to call Kenny "the ice cream kid." The nickname began to catch on around school.

Every day Kenny wished that Mrs. Merrin would come back, so Max would come back, too. He still believed that Max could help him get his part back from Brian.

Finally, on Monday, things got back to normal when Mrs. Merrin returned.

"It's good to be back. I think all of you must have grown at least five inches while I was gone," Mrs. Merrin said. She was sitting on her desk, smiling at everyone. "I got so lonely for you that I started giving my puppy detentions."

The class laughed.

"Did you get our cards, Mrs. Merrin?" asked Melissa.

"Yes. I loved every one of them," the teacher answered. "But there was one that wasn't signed and I couldn't figure out who sent it. It said, 'Hope you get well and make the school scene quick. Your staying home is making me sicksville.' Who wrote that one?"

No one raised a hand, which didn't surprise Jeffrey and Kenny. That card could only have come from the third-grade ghost!

Mrs. Merrin shrugged and said, "Well, never mind. Now we've got to get into high gear with our class play. Ready or not, it's showtime tomorrow."

"You mean it's show*down* time," Kenny said, looking over at Brian Carr. But where was Max?

A few minutes later, the third-graders were in the auditorium ready to rehearse. The scenery was in place onstage. And it looked just like the park across the street from the school. It even had one very large pine tree, just like the tree where Kenny first saw Max.

On Melissa's signal, the rehearsal began. Four kids walked onstage. This time the four were played by Jeffrey, Ricky, Becky Singer, and Kenny.

"I thought I saw a spaceship land in those trees over there," announced Becky Singer in her loud, clear voice.

"It looks like an alien from another planet," Jeffrey said. "Where do you think it landed?"

Kenny pointed to a tree. In his new role, he had a lot to do, but he didn't have anything to say.

Then it was time for Brian Carr to make his entrance. He was supposed to step out from behind the tree and speak his first line—the line Kenny had never managed to say when he was the alien.

Kenny looked around. Why wasn't Max there? Didn't he know that this was their last chance to make Brian Carr lose the part? Couldn't Max at least keep one promise—an important one like this one?

Just then, Brian stepped out from behind the tree. But as he walked forward, he fell over, face first. He stood up, but he wasn't up for long. His feet went straight out from under him again. This time he landed loudly on his bottom. Brian tried it again, but it was as though he were trying to stand up on a slanted ice rink. He fell again and again.

Everyone was so surprised that they didn't know what to do. Finally Melissa couldn't help it. She burst out laughing.

"Brian," Mrs. Merrin said, "unless the play has changed drastically since I've been gone, I think you're supposed to be an alien from outer space. Not a slapstick clown from outer space."

"Mrs. Merrin, it wasn't me. Somebody's pushing me and knocking me down," Brian said, looking around for the wise guy.

Everyone else looked around, too. But no one could see anyone standing anywhere near Brian.

Jeffrey smiled at Kenny, and Kenny gave Jeffrey a thumbs-up sign. Max had come through!

But then Jeffrey noticed that Ben and Melissa were both watching him very hard.

Jeffrey gulped. He had seen that look before and he knew exactly where, too. It was the look Kenny had had on his face when he started to believe that there really was a ghost.

Melissa finally turned her attention back to Brian. "Brian," she said, "say your lines."

Ricky, Jeffrey, Becky, and Kenny took their places and started looking afraid of Brian. Jeffrey gave Brian his cue.

"It looks like an alien from another planet," Jeffrey said. "Where do you think it landed?"

Kenny pointed at Brian. Brian stepped forward. But the minute he opened his mouth, a telephone began to ring.

"What's the joke?" Mrs. Merrin said. "There is no telephone in the auditorium."

Suddenly Brian began tearing at his shirt with his hands. He acted as if there were something

inside. Then he reached into his shirt and pulled out the receiver of a telephone, still attached to a long, twisty cord.

"Brian, what on earth are you doing?" asked Mrs. Merrin. She had to speak loudly to be heard above the laughter.

"He must be making long-distance calls back to his planet," Jeffrey said.

"That's not in my script!" Ben protested from the first row.

"Ben can forget his script," Kenny whispered to Jeffrey. "Max is writing his own now."

"Listen, guys," Mrs. Merrin announced. "This is a lot of fun, but tomorrow is coming closer every minute."

"Let's try this scene again," called Melissa, the director.

Once more, Kenny pointed at Brian.

Brian took two big alien steps toward the four

frightened Earthlings. They were watching his every move. He put his hands on his hips, opened his mouth, and began to speak. And that's when the most amazing thing of all happened. Out of Brian's mouth came . . . not words, but bubbles. Big, round, soppy, soapy bubbles. Jeffrey couldn't see how Max was doing it, but it was a great effect.

"Brian, I would like to have a student-teacher conference with you at your earliest convenience—which better be right this minute," Mrs. Merrin said. Everyone could see that part of her was laughing. But part of her was not.

She and Brian met in the back of the auditorium for a moment. When they came back, Brian was no longer going to play the alien. She had had enough of his jokes.

"We've got a tough situation here, gang," Mrs. Merrin said. "The play is tomorrow. The whole school will be here. All of the parents will be here. But we don't have an alien. Does anyone else want to try to learn the part overnight?"

Once again Kenny's hand shot up into the air so fast that his feet practically left the ground.

"Oh, no. Not again, Max," Jeffrey mumbled.

Just then, Max made himself visible. But he wasn't standing next to Kenny, raising his hand.

He was sitting out in the audience. Jeffrey's head jerked around toward Kenny. What? Kenny was raising his hand on his own!

"Mrs. Merrin. Mrs. Merrin!" Kenny said excitedly. "Give me another chance. Please."

"Kenny . . ." The teacher paused to think of how to finish her sentence.

"But I know all of the lines and I can do it. I know I can."

Mrs. Merrin looked carefully at Kenny's face and then at everyone in the class. "All right. I'll give you one more chance," she said.

Kenny and Brian changed places one more time. Becky, Ricky, and Jeffrey came out onstage and Brian stood next to Jeffrey.

"I've heard of washing your mouth out with soap," Jeffrey whispered. "But you were awesome, Brian."

"Oh, shut up," Brian snapped. "All I know is somehow this was all Kenny Thompsen's fault. And I'll tell you one thing: I'm never going to get into another fight with that dude. He's totally bad."

This time, Brian pointed at Kenny while Becky said, "I thought I saw a spaceship land in those trees over there."

Then Jeffrey said his lines.

Then Brian pointed.

Then Kenny stepped forward.

Everyone stopped breathing. They had been here before, watching Kenny and waiting for him to say his lines. But could he do it now?

"HELLO, EARTHLINGS!" Kenny's voice boomed out of his mouth and into the auditorium. The echo seemed to ring forever. "DO NOT BE AFRAID OF ME, EARTHLINGS," Kenny continued. "I HAVE BROUGHT YOU AN IMPORTANT MESSAGE OF PEACE FROM OUTER SPACE. AND A BETTER WAY TO GET YOUR GREASY POTS AND PANS CLEAN! I BRING YOU GREETINGS FROM THE PLANET OF A THOUSAND AND ONE COMMERCIALS!"

Suddenly, the curtain came down and music began to play. The lights in the auditorium flashed on and off.

"Whoever is playing with the controls backstage better stop it right now!" Melissa shouted.

Jeffrey ran backstage before anyone else got there. Max was sitting at the control panel. He was pushing buttons and pulling levers. "Hey, Daddy-o, like, there sure are a lot of crazy buttons to push back here."

"Max, get away from there. You're ruining our rehearsal," Jeffrey said.

62

"Cool out a minute, Jeffrey. I'm learning what all these buttons do," Max said.

"Not now," Jeffrey said.

"Not now? Then when?" The ghost looked very innocent. "Because I mean, like, you don't want me to push the wrong button and make a mistake *during* the play tomorrow, do you? That would be totally uncool!"

Chapter Seven

Friday was play day. Everyone backstage was nervous. The auditorium seats were filling up fast. Soon all of the parents and all of the other students in the school would be sitting out front.

Becky Singer paced backstage. "Don't anybody step on my new white shoes," she announced. "They've got to be clean for the play."

"Mrs. Merrin, could I say my part at two-thirty?" asked Jenny Arthur. Jenny Arthur had been chosen to introduce the play. "My parents probably can't get here until then. I don't want them to miss me."

"I know how you feel, Jenny," Mrs. Merrin said, "but you're supposed to welcome the audience. We can't have you doing that after the play has started."

Kenny pulled Jeffrey aside. Kenny was wearing his alien costume: green pants, green T-shirt, a third eye pasted on his chin, and a Chicago Cubs cap. The cap was Kenny's idea.

"I hope Max gets here," Kenny said to Jeffrey. "I don't see him yet. But he promised to do something special."

Jeffrey sighed. "You don't know him that well yet. Things might go smoother if he *doesn't* show up."

At exactly two o'clock, the lights in the auditorium dimmed. The audience grew quiet and eager. Jenny Arthur stepped out from behind the curtain and walked to a microphone at the side of the stage. She stood in the middle of a bright spotlight beam.

"Parents, teachers, and students," she began. But as she welcomed everyone, the spotlight began to move to the left. Jenny moved over to follow it and stay in the light. "The story you're about to see hasn't happened. But it might." The light kept moving, so Jenny kept moving, but she kept talking, too. The spotlight led Jenny from one side of the stage to the other. It wouldn't hold still.

"Something weird is going on," Kenny whispered backstage.

"It's just Max telling us that he's here," Jeffrey answered.

"Good," Kenny said, smiling.

Finally Jenny finished her speech. "We hope

this play gives you something to laugh about and something to think about," she said. Then the spotlight went out—before Jenny got off the stage! "I can't see where I'm going!" she shouted in the dark.

Everyone waited until Jenny found her way off the stage.

Then the curtain went up and the play began. Once more, Jeffrey, Ricky, Becky Singer, and Brian Carr came walking through the park that had been painted onstage.

"I thought I saw a spaceship land in those trees over there," Becky said.

"It looks like an alien from another planet," Jeffrey said. "Where do you think it landed?"

Brian Carr pointed and then Kenny stepped out from behind a painted tree and made his entrance. As soon as the four humans saw him, they moved away in fear.

"Hello, Earthlings! Do not be afraid of me, Earthlings!" said Kenny in a loud voice.

"Why not?" asked Jeffrey. "You just grew another eye."

Max had just decided that an alien needed *four* eyes and pasted a new sticker right in the middle of Kenny's forehead. Kenny's mouth

opened soundlessly. It took him a moment before he could go on with the play.

"Earthlings, I have brought you an important
message of peace from outer space," Kenny
said. "And a better way to get your greasy pots
and pans clean. I bring you greetings from the
Planet of a Thousand and One Commercials."

"Never heard of it," Jeffrey said. "Where is it?"

"You can't miss it," Kenny answered. "Just
hang a right at the Galaxy of Silly T-shirts, then
go three light-years and one heavy year until
you come to the Cowboy Constellation. That's
where all the 'shooting stars' come from. Then
take a left at the all-night doughnut shop and
you're there. Come early and stay late. Plenty
of free parking."

"Sounds like a cool place," Ricky said.

"I was hoping you'd say that," Kenny said.
"Earthlings, for a limited time only, you, too,
can have an all-expenses-paid vacation to the
Planet of a Thousand and One Commercials."

"Really?" asked Jeffrey. "When?"

"How about right now!" the alien said. He
threw a net around Jeffrey and the three others.

"Hey, wait!" Jeffrey yelled. "What about
baseball practice?"

67

"Yeah, and what about my karate lesson?" asked Ricky.

"And what about getting our parents to sign permission slips?" Brian asked. "We can't go on a field trip without permission slips."

"Too bad! I can't wait!" Kenny shouted. "You are all coming with me back to my planet immediately." Then the curtain came down.

Backstage, everyone scrambled to change the set for Act Two. Five minutes later, the curtain went up again.

Now Arvin Pubbler was standing in the middle of the stage all by himself. He was wearing a shirt, a tie, and a sport jacket. He gave the audience a big smile and said, "How would you like to win a million dollars? Or a new car? Or half a ton of canned chili? Well, you can if you know the right answers. Anything's possible on the Planet of a Thousand and One Commercials. And here come our new contestants now!"

Then Kenny led Jeffrey, Becky, Ricky, and Brian onto the stage. They were still trapped in his net. Kenny took the net off the four Earthlings.

"Why did you bring us here?" Jeffrey asked.

"Because you must be contestants on our game show," Kenny explained. "Everyone else

68

on the planet has already been on the show. Without contestants, we cannot have commercials. And as you know, this is the Planet of a Thousand and One Commercials! The game show must go on!"

"But I want to go home," Brian Carr whined.

"You will," Kenny replied. "But only *if* you answer the questions correctly. Otherwise, you must stay here to be contestants forever."

Arvin Pubbler stepped forward. The rest of the class came out dressed all in green like Kenny. They sat down on the stage like an audience.

"It's time to play our game!" Arvin shouted. "Earthlings, come on down!"

Kenny pushed the four Earth visitors toward a table. There were buzzers on the table that Ben, the scientist, had rigged up for the play. There were also four chairs.

The alien audience cheered wildly as the four Earthlings sat down at the table.

"Okay, here's your first question," Arvin said. "What's round on the ends and high in the middle?"

Ricky pressed his buzzer first. "Everyone knows that old joke. The answer is Ohio."

"I'm sorry, but that's wrong," Arvin said.

"Wrong? I've known that joke since I was a little kid!" Ricky said. "You know—Ohio has two *O*'s on the ends and *HI* in the middle."

"Not on this planet," Arvin said. "The correct answer is Mother Fletcher's Mashed Potatoes on Wheels. That's right! Only Mother Fletcher's Mashed Potatoes are piled high in the middle and then they're put on round wheels, so you can take them anywhere. Buy some today."

Jeffrey, Becky, Ricky, and Brian squirmed in their seats.

"I'll have your next question right after this commercial," Arvin said.

Then Mary Louise Slimak came out onstage. She asked the audience, "Have you tried Smear Detergent? It's the only detergent that puts mud and grass stains *on* your clothes. So buy Smear— the detergent for kids who are too busy watching TV commercials to get dirty."

"And now back to the game," Arvin went on. "Here's your next question. What do these things have in common? A flashlight, a pen with twelve colors of ink, a glow-in-the-dark yo-yo, dinosaur-egg stickers, and a remote-controlled race car?"

Becky pressed her buzzer quickly. "That's all

70

stuff Benjamin Hyde got for his birthday," she guessed.

"Wrong," Arvin Pubbler shouted. "All of those things are in specially marked boxes of Wacky Ducky Cereal! Kids love it because inside every box they find a mountain of prizes! In fact, there are so many prizes in the box, there's no room for any cereal. Buy some today! Only fifty-two dollars at your favorite toy store."

"I want to go home," Becky said.

"No problem," said Kenny. "Order today. Call this toll-free number. Friendly operators are standing by right now!"

Jeffrey, Becky, Ricky, and Brian held their ears. "Stop!" they shouted. "All of your commercials are driving us crazy!"

Suddenly the lights went out. Jeffrey stayed onstage while everyone else ran off. He lay down on the floor with a pillow.

Then a small lamp flickered on. Jeffrey pretended to wake up from a deep sleep. He looked around and shook his head. "I'm in my own room," he said. "It was all a dream. I was just having a bad dream. Or was I?"

At that point, right before the curtain came down for the end of the play, Kenny, the alien, was supposed to walk across the stage to prove

that it *wasn't* a dream. However, Max had been
saving the best for last.

To Jeffrey's surprise, and to everyone else's
amazement, Kenny didn't walk across the stage.
He *flew*! With Max holding on to him tightly,
Kenny circled around Jeffrey once. Then Max
and Kenny flew to the other side of the stage
before disappearing from sight.

The audience gasped and held their breath.
So did Jeffrey. He knew that he was going to
have a lot of explaining to do after this one.

When the curtain came down for the last time,
the applause from the students and parents was
thunderous. The class took one bow after an-

other. And then came the special bows. Mrs. Merrin was first. Then she introduced Melissa as the play's director; Ben, as the play's writer; and Kenny, as the play's star.

After that everyone mobbed Kenny. They seemed to have forgotten the first twenty minutes of the play and only wanted to talk about the last ten seconds of it.

Kenny couldn't stop laughing and grinning long enough to answer, not even when Mrs. Merrin gently pushed her way to the front of the crowd.

"Kenny," she said, "how on earth did you do that?"

Jeffrey spoke up first and fast. "Special effects, Mrs. Merrin," he said.

"But I didn't see any strings."

"Uh, well, Mrs. Merrin, Kenny can't really explain it."

"You can say that again," Kenny added.

"Uh," stammered Jeffrey, looking around, "you'd have to ask Ben."

"Ask *Ben*?" everyone said. Even Ben said it.

"Well, it's one of Ben's scientific experiments," explained Jeffrey. "But I forgot. He can't talk about it—not until he gets it patented."

"Jeffrey!" Ben protested, "you know I—"

"I *know* you want to tell them, Ben," Jeffrey said, poking him hard in the ribs. Then, just to make sure, he clamped his hand over Ben's mouth. "But, remember, you promised the president you wouldn't tell."

When it was all over, Jeffrey and Kenny walked home with Melissa, Ben, and Ricky. Jeffrey tried to explain Kenny's flying scene, but his friends just weren't buying it.

"Special effects?" Ricky said.

"Scientific experiment?" Ben said.

"Baloney," Melissa said.

Ben put his arm around Jeffrey's shoulders. "Jeffrey, you know that story you kept telling us at the beginning of the year? The one about finding a ghost in your desk?"

"The story we always laughed at and never believed," Ricky said.

"Tell it to us one more time," Melissa urged. "We're really interested now."

Jeffrey looked at Kenny. "Oh, boy," Jeffrey said. "Here we go again, Max!"

Here's a peek at Jeffrey's next adventure with Max, the third-grade ghost!

MAX SAVES THE DAY

"You know what I was thinking when Ricky and that new kid Robin Dessart were starting to fight?" Kenny asked.

"Of course I know," Jeffrey said. "I can read minds." He pressed his thumbs lightly against his forehead. "Go ahead and tell me. I'll see if I got it right."

I was thinking too bad Max wasn't here," Kenny replied.

"That's exactly what I thought you were thinking."

Kenny continued, "I wanted Max to be here because he would have stopped the fight."

"Max stop a fight? He would have sold tickets," Jeffrey said with a laugh as he started to walk home.

"But Max is definitely on our side," Kenny insisted.

After taking a few more steps, Jeffrey stopped. Kenny could tell that he was getting an idea.

"What's your idea?" he asked Jeffrey. "Tell me."

"It's what you said," Jeffrey answered. "About Max. Maybe I can convince him to play a trick on Robin. But first, I've got to *find* him."

ABOUT THE AUTHORS

Bill and Megan Stine have written numerous books for young readers, including titles in these series: *The Cranberry Cousins; Wizards, Warriors, and You; The Three Investigators; Indiana Jones; G.I. Joe;* and *Jem.* They live on New York City's Upper West Side with their seven-year-old son, Cody, who believes in ghosts.